Copyright ©1993 A.E.T. Browne & Partners
All rights reserved
First published in Great Britain 1993
by Julia MacRae
an imprint of Random House
20 Vauxhall Bridge Road, London SW1V 2SA

Random House Australia (Pty) Ltd
20 Alfred Street, Milsons Point, Sydney, NSW 2061

Random House New Zealand Ltd
18 Poland Road, Glenfield, Auckland, New Zealand

Random House South Africa (Pty) Ltd
PO Box 337, Bergvlei, 2012, South Africa

Printed in Hong Kong

British Library Cataloguing-in-Publication Data.
A catalogue record for this book is available
from the British Library.

ISBN 1-85681-037-2

The Big Baby

A Little Joke

A N T H O N Y   B R O W N E

Julia MacRae Books

LONDON SYDNEY AUCKLAND JOHANNESBURG

Everyone said that John Young's dad was young for his age.

He did have young clothes,

and young hairstyles.

He liked very loud pop music,

and he had a whole den full of toys.

Mr Young liked being young,
and so he tried to stay that way.
Every morning he cycled.
(Well, *nearly* every morning...
well... sometimes.)

And he spent AGES and AGES in the bathroom.

When people said to him,
"You do look *young* for your age,"
Mr Young grinned boyishly.
John's mum just smiled.
"You should look after *yourself*
a bit more, Mum," he said.
But whenever *he* had a headache,
or caught a slight cold, he made a
BIG fuss, went to bed, and called it 'flu.

Mrs Young called him a Big Baby.

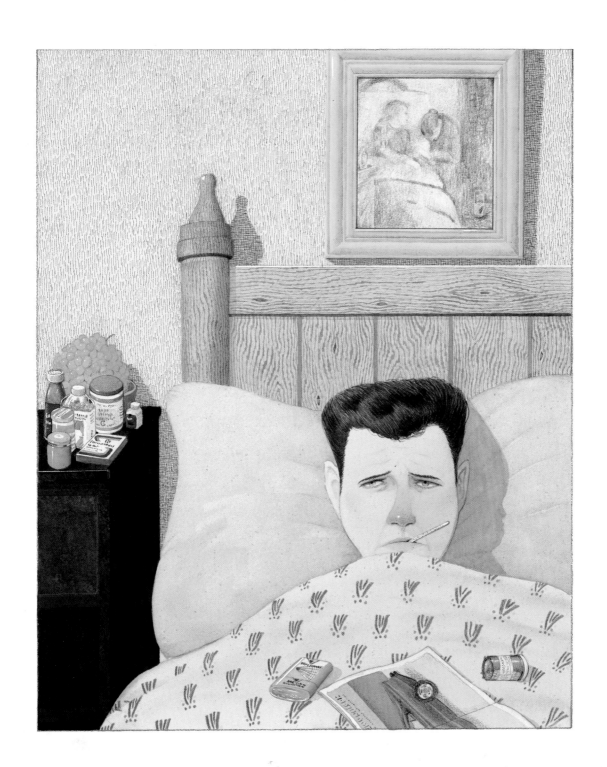

One evening he came home bursting with
excitement. He was always buying new pills
and special foods from health shops, and that day
he'd found a strange little shop in a back street
that sold the most amazing tonic drink.

It was called ELIXA DE YOOF, and that night he eagerly drank the whole bottle.

Well, John's very fond of his dad really,
but when his mum called him into their bedroom
the next morning, John just burst out laughing.
There in bed with his mother was a baby –
with his dad's face!

"He's *really* done it now, hasn't he?"
said Mrs Young, and there was just a
little bit of a smile on her face too.

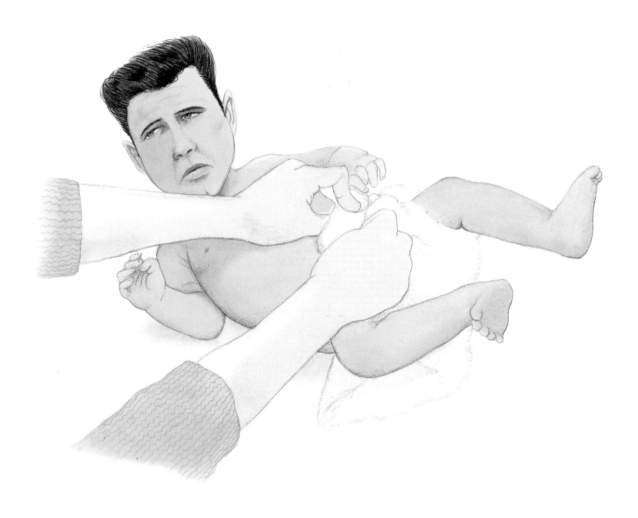

"The first thing we must do is put a nappy
on him, he's soaking," she said. "John, can you
get one from the bottom drawer while I clean
him up?" Mr Young tried to say something, but
all he came out with was, "Ga-ga-ga-gaaa."

Afterwards Mrs Young carried him downstairs
for breakfast, and John fetched his old high-chair
from the basement. His dad made a real mess
of his muesli.

They took him for a walk later, and everyone stopped and made a big fuss of him.

He didn't seem to enjoy that much. John's
mum had to say that he was a friend's baby,
and she was looking after him. Mr Young tried
to say something, but all they could hear
was, "Boggaboggabogga."

When they got back home, Mrs Young changed
his nappy.

John tried playing with him and very carefully
built him a tower, but as usual Mr Young didn't
seem interested in playing with his son.

He cried and cried so Mrs Young sat him on the
potty, but it didn't help. Poor Mr Young
looked so silly that John felt quite sorry for him.

John's mum put his dad to bed
and he slept for hours.

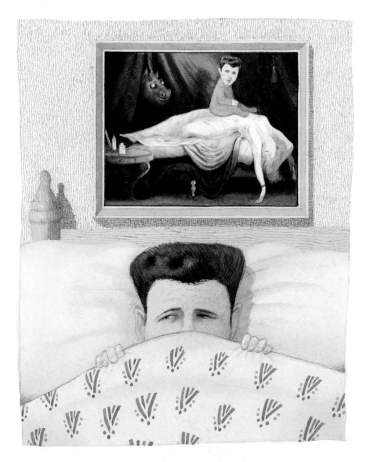

Much later they heard Mr Young's 'poorly' voice,
"C-can you come upstairs?"
They dashed up into his room.
There was John's dad, back to normal.
"I've had a TERRIBLE dream," he wailed.
"Oh, poor baby," said Mrs Young.
"But how did *you* know?" asked Mr Young.
She looked at John and smiled.
"Hey, Dad!" said John. "Go and look in the mirror."

And he saw his first grey hair.